Miss Einstein

AKCHARA MUKUNTHU

MISS EINSTEIN

To my family and friends – people and animals.
Especially my grandmother, Mekala, who taught me my
very first words. I could not have written this book
without you!

MISS EINSTEIN

CONTENTS

MISS EINSTEIN

ACKNOWLEDGMENTS

Special thanks to my parents for reviewing this book and encouraging me through the whole process. Without their support and guidance, this book would not have been possible.

And also, I am grateful to my sister for encouraging me with her kind words.

CHAPTER 1
THE LONG MONDAY

"If you dream it, you can do it."- *Walt Disney*

"The answer to number eight is x=41," Mrs. Bobbins announces, in her teacher's voice.

I, Ella Teren, have gotten all the questions correct so far, as usual. Not to brag, but I'm smart and especially good at math. My parents left me when I was small, so Aunt Sandra, and Uncle Evon are my guardians.

Once, I asked Aunt Sandra, "How am I naturally good at math?"

"Well, your parents were both geniuses in the area," she replied.

Since they were mathematicians, my theory is that math is "in my blood."

My friends are the nicest friends you can find! Their names are Cari and Milly. Cari will always cheer you up when you are down in the dumps, and Milly is a person you can rely on when you're in need. We've been friends for as long as I can remember!

There's one thing that's not too obvious about me: math is not my favorite subject! I'm telling you the truth, science is. It's not only my favorite subject, but it's my favorite thing in the whole universe!

When I was younger, I asked Uncle Evon, "I like science more than math, so will Mom and Dad be mad at me if I don't follow their footsteps?"

"Of course not, honey. They'll be happy if you're happy, and believe it or not, there's a lot of math involved in science," he replied.

I'm looking forward to science class because our science teacher, Mr. Peso, told us that we're going to be doing an investigation related to physics. I absolutely love physics!

"And that's the last problem. Students, please proceed to your next class," Mrs. Bobbins instructs.

This is when everyone goes over to their friends and they chat before heading to their lockers to get their textbooks. Boy, it's loud! I usually go straight to my locker (which fortunately is right in between Cari and Milly's lockers) and chat with my best friends for one or two minutes, and that's exactly what I'm planning on doing today.

Once we finish talking, we walk to Mr. Peso's science room. We're lucky to have all our classes together except math, since it's so rare to even have a few classes with your friends let alone most of them. Mr. Peso is hilarious! He can make jokes about anything. Class is also super-fun with him because he lets us experiment, unlike other teachers who literally tell us how to do everything and don't let us have fun or give us even a tiny-weeny bit of freedom!

Yesterday, Mr. Peso told us, "Students, tomorrow we are going to be doing a fun physics investigation."

Durkin, the boy that all the teachers adore, asked, "Mr. Peso, what is the investigation?"

Mr. Peso replied, "Can't tell you, kiddo. It's a surprise."

Mr. Peso's students are always longing to hear those very words - surprise investigations are the best! In the fall when we were doing chemistry, we got to make elephant toothpaste, and slime!

As we take our seats, Mr. Peso requests for a drumroll, "Students, today we are going to do a… pendulum investigation!" he says, loudly, waking all of the half-asleep students up.

Yay, I love pendulums! When I was six, Aunt Sandra and I were going shopping at the mall for my birthday. We went to the super cool science store, F.K.S.S. (Fun Kiddy Science Store). When we stepped in there, I was so jubilant.

"Ella, dear, you can pick out one thing - anything - as your birthday present," she told me.

I immediately searched the whole store for the best possible present. I finally found something; it was a pendulum. It looked so satisfying and mesmerizing!

Right away, I took it up to Aunt Sandra and squealed, "Aunt Sandra, this is what I want!"

"Okay, let me check the price," she replied as she turned the box to check the price sticker on the bottom.

Once she saw it, her eyes were as big as saucers!

"Yikes," she mumbled, "I'm afraid I can't afford this. You can pick out any other thing."

"You lied to me!" I scowled.

"What?" she asked, bewildered.

"You said I could pick anything. And now you're saying I can't?" I asked.

I don't know about you, but it seemed like a valuable question to me – and still does.

My heart felt like it was being shattered into a million pieces!

I ran out of the store and Aunt Sandra followed, yelling, "Wait, Ella, wait!"

That night, Aunt Sandra, and Uncle Evon were whispering in the kitchen. I only caught my name here and there.

Then, they gave me the talk about how I can't get everything I want. "I only want one pendulum. It's not much!" I cried in my head.

Finally, my chance is here to utilize this fascinating object. I want to make the best of the time I get to experiment with it.

Mr. Peso announces that the homework for tonight is a worksheet on the investigation and I ask, "Mr. Peso, can I borrow a pendulum, so I can further investigate?"

"Of course, Ella. I love your enthusiasm! Just be sure to bring it back in good condition," he reminds me.

"I will!" I reply.

I'm so ecstatic to show Aunt Sandra and Uncle Evon the pendulum!

Funny story, a few days ago, Uncle Evon asked me, "Ella, did I ever tell you that I had science *without* experiments in middle school?"

"That's so sad, Uncle Evon! We have science *with* experiments now. This cool man named Mr. Peso teaches us," I replied.

"Oh, well, I'm still the coolest man according to you, right?" he joked.

"Of course!" I assured.

After science, it's third period. We have ELA (English Language Arts) with Ms. Domo. In a nutshell, it's reading, and writing combined with a bit of public speaking. I guess I'm fairly good at it.

Ms. Domo is a high-spirited teacher who is good-natured to everyone. She gives us engaging projects, and the homework in her class is not boring at all.

"Welcome class! Happy Monday! How are you this lovely day?" Ms. Domo asks as we all get settled in.

The room is filled with the usual mixed responses, "Meh", "Bad", "Okay", "Horrible", "Fine", and an occasional, "Good".

"What are we doing today?" Ameli asks.

She's like Durkin; she asks the exact same question every, single day. There's at least one person in every period that's like them.

"Good question, Ameli. Today we're going to learn about biographies," Ms. Domo asks, "Can anyone tell me what a biography is?"

She calls on me, "Ella," she says.

"A biography is when a different person writes about someone's life," I tell the class.

"Nicely worded, Ella!" she praises.

"Everyone think. What is one person that you admire and look up to, your role model, someone you'd like to write a biography about?" she asks.

I would choose the great, Albert Einstein. He achieved a ton of things in science, especially in physics, and that's what I tend to do.

"Give me a thumbs-up when you're done," Ms. Domo directs.

That's why some people don't like her. She's into cheesy things like high-fives, fist-bumps, and thumbs-ups. I don't really mind, though. She's a great teacher and that's all that matters. I mean even Uncle Evon does things that are embarrassing at times, but I still do love him.

Since Ms. Domo is a teacher, someone who you must listen to, everyone gives Ms. Domo thumbs-ups.

Ms. Domo looks around the room and tells us, "You can start jotting down your ideas about your role model in your notebooks."

I take out my brown notebook. This is not just any brown though – it's obnoxious. It's the kind of brown that makes you want to say, "Ugh!"

Aunt Sandra got it for me from the clearance section at Imli's Inexpensive Items. The pages are a lighter, more disgusting shade of brown. But I still write in it - an awful notebook is better than no notebook at all, right?

I take out my pencil and start writing down my ideas. that we do some activities on biographies until the end of the period. Now you know that the mornings are too hard on us - or actually not yet! There's still fourth period (and I'm already drained)!

Fourth period is Social Studies. Normally, I enjoy learning, but even I think Social Studies is boring, not to be mean though. And that concludes the long morning.

After our tiresome morning, we get to relax because it's time for lunch. Lunch is most people's favorite, but not mine. Aunt Sandra always packs me a PB&J sandwich. The sad thing about schools in our area is that the school lunches are expensive. In elementary school, Aunt Sandra packed a variety of lunches, but now, because middle school starts earlier, she only has time to pack a PB&J sandwich!

At lunch, Cari, Milly, and I talk about our weekends. That's what we do every, single Monday at lunch. It's kind of routine. Milly always complains about something that happened with her little brother, Marky. She thinks that he's a complete nuisance (I feel for her). Meanwhile, Cari's parents do fun things with her.

"Guess what I did this weekend?" Cari asks.

"What?" Milly and I ask at the same time.

"My parents and I went on an all-you-can-buy shopping spree!" Cari replies, with joy.

After reading the previous statement, you might think that Cari is a spoiled brat. Well, you're half-right. Is she spoiled? Kind of. Is she a brat? Not at all. So there!

"You're so lucky, Cari! I had to get stuck with my brother all weekend. It was torture!" Milly cries, and she goes on and on about how Marky tried to squirt glue in her hair!

After Milly finishes complaining about Marky, Cari asks me, "You seem oddly silent, Ella. How was your weekend?"

First of all, I'm silent, but I don't think that it's odd. Secondly, I like it when they talk, and I listen.

"It was fine. Aunt Sandra had a lot of open-houses to go to and I got to go with her," I utter, plainly.

"That's nice," Milly replies.

Cari agrees.

That's when the bell rings. We're off to our lockers to get ready for my favorite part of school: electives. Yay!

Cari, Milly, and I have a secret system for electives. Listen, I'm only telling you this because I trust you.

Our system is that each year in middle school we have three trimesters of electives. There are nine trimesters in all, and three of us, so each year each of us will get to choose the elective for all of us for one of the trimesters. If that's confusing, I know. It took us a while to get used to it.

Also, luckily, in our middle school you get what you want for your electives, no matter what, but it's 'first come-first served'.

This trimester it's Cari's turn. Cari really likes art, especially sewing, so we all signed up for the sewing elective. It's fun to do things as friends, so we created this system.

Now you shouldn't tell *anyone* about this.

After lunch, we grab our sewing supplies and head to the art room.

As we enter the art room, we see that not many kids had arrived. I check the cerulean-blue wall clock. We're early.

Our sewing elective teacher, also known as Alexi's mom, Mrs. Parke is writing on some papers. She's one of the best parent chaperones.

"Hello, Mrs. Parke," we all chorus.

"Hello, girls. Have a seat," she replies.

For sewing class, we sit at round tables big enough to seat three people.

Once kids start arriving, Mrs. Parke greets, "Welcome, students. Today, we're going to sew mini pillows."

I've always wanted to sew pillows! Mrs. Parke carefully teaches us step-by-step.

"Students, it's just about time for you to go wherever you go after school," she announces once everyone finishes.

She also requests for us to give her our pillows. I made a leopard-print pillow. Cari made a chevron-print one. And Milly made a paisley-print one. They all look really good!

We gather all our stuff from our lockers and start talking about our plans after school. Aunt Sandra and Uncle Evon usually work late. When I was in elementary school, they would send me to Audrey's After School. Audrey picked us up at our elementary school and drove us to her nice and cozy house. I liked it there because if you didn't want to do the activities you could just do your homework. I did all the activities when I was little, but as I got older, I would usually just get a head start on my homework.

CHAPTER 2
AFTERSCHOOL ADVENTURES

"If people are doubting how far you can go, go so far that you can't hear them anymore."- Michele Ruiz

Today, Milly has badminton tryouts for the school badminton team (yeah, we have one), at the school field. Cari and I decide to stay to cheer her on.

I need to call Aunt Sandra or Uncle Evon to let them know about my plans. I don't have a phone yet because Aunt Sandra and Uncle Evon think that I'm not old enough, or at least that's what they keep on telling me. I borrow Cari's cool smartphone and call Aunt Sandra.

Aunt Sandra picks up and asks, "Is this Ella?"

"Yeah. Can I stay at the school field for Milly's badminton tryouts?" I ask.

"Sure. I'll come pick you up at 6," she asks.

"Great, bye!" I reply.

After the call, I hand the phone to Cari and we walk together to the bleachers next to where the tryouts are happening.

The name Milly might sound like it belongs to a girl with a frilly dress and ribbons in her hair, but I can guarantee that you will never, ever see Milly wearing frilly dresses or ribbons of any sort.

She is an athlete. Milly is especially awesome at badminton. She has speed, powerful arms, and perfect hand-eye coordination. That's what Coach Filomena, Sandy Brooks' PE teacher says. Milly is doing good so far. The kids who went before her were good, but not as good as the Mill-Monster.

That's the nickname Cari and I made up for her.

Well, now her tryout is over.

"You did brilliant! It was magical!" Coach Filomena compliments.

Milly blushes as she thanks her.

Afterwards, Cari and I overload her with compliments.

Milly takes a sip of her sparkling water and tells us, "You guys can stop now."

She goes up to Coach Filomena and asks, "When are you going to post the results?"

"In a bit. You can stay here and wait, or you can come back tomorrow," Coach Filomena replies.

Milly thanks her again and comes back to the bench that we're sitting on.

"We stay here?" she asks.

"Yep!" Cari and I reply.

Milly's sweating, so she says, "I'm going to go shower, you two, wait here."

We nod. Milly quickly grabs her wisteria-purple sports bag. She enters the gym door and vanishes. Our school has showers in the bathrooms.

Cari gets a call, she hands the phone to me as she says, "It's your aunt."

I grab the phone and press the accept button. I place the phone up to my ear.

Aunt Sandra exclaims, "Ella, I'm getting a promotion. I'm a real-estate agent manager. I get to manage other agents!"

"That's so exciting, Aunt Sandra. I'm happy for you!" I reply.

"And there's more. Your uncle and I are going to pick you up in 30 minutes and we can all go out for pizza," she tells me.

I'm so surprised. We haven't gone out to eat in a long time. Aunt Sandra always manages to feed us a home-cooked dinner. They are usually leftovers, though. I guess I'll tell them about the pendulum when they come to pick me up.

While she's showering, Cari shows me some pictures on her phone. We also take some selfies together. As always, the one with our silly faces is the most hilarious one. We laugh so much our cheeks and stomachs start hurting. We even fall to the floor and guffaw!

We're still laughing when Milly arrives.

"Hey, guys. I'm back. What's so funny?" she asks.

Cari holds up her phone for Milly to look at.

"Guys, that's…," she could not even finish her sentence because she fell onto the shamrock-green grass and started guffawing just like us.

We're still laughing when Aunt Sandra and Uncle Evon come over to the benches.

Aunt Sandra always wears formal clothes and heels with apricot tights. She also always wears make-up.

Uncle Evon is not the kind of guy who wears a suit and tie. He is always the chill-type and his clothes show. He is the total opposite of Aunt Sandra, but they somehow get along.

Aunt Sandra and Uncle Evon's clothes don't change my impression on them at all. I love them and always will.

"Ahem," Aunt Sandra harrumphs, trying to get our attention.

"Hi, Aunt Sandra. Hi, Uncle Evon," I greet.

Milly and Cari wave.

"Are you ready to go?" Uncle Evon asks.

"Yeah," I reply.

I grab my backpack.

"Bye, guys!" I say to Milly and Cari as we walk towards our beige car.

"Bye!" they say back.

My mouth waters the whole walk to the car. The distance between the field and the parking lot is huge!

When we finally reach our car, I open the door and enter.

We're all buckled up and Uncle Evon is pulling out the car right now.

I ask, "Which pizza place are we going to?"

"Your choice!" Aunt Sandra replies, happily.

"No, you should choose. It's your special day," I insist.

"Oh, thanks! How about Pami's Pizzeria?" she asks.

"Sounds good," I reply.

We've only been there once for my fifth birthday. The pizza is simply divine.

The car ride starts out good. We talk about our days, like usual. I remember about the pendulum.

"Aunt Sandra, Uncle Evon, I have something to tell you," I start.

"What is it, Ella?" Uncle Evon asks.

"Remember the incident when I was six, and I wanted a pendulum, but I couldn't get one?" I ask.

They both look at each other, sigh, and reply, "Yes," at the same time.

"Well, Mr. Peso let me take one of the pendulums from our class investigation home to experiment with!" I exclaim.

"That's amazing!" Aunt Sandra replies.

"Yeah, you shouldn't let this opportunity go to waste!" Uncle Evon advises.

"I know. It seems as if today is my lucky day," I say.

"Mines too," Aunt Sandra chimes in.

"Mines too," Uncle Evon adds.

Aunt Sandra and I put on our "Really?" faces.

"What? I get pizza. That's considered a lucky day in my world," Uncle Evon reasons.

Aunt Sandra and I laugh.

We finally get there and walk into Pami's
Pizzeria (with a whole lot of hunger). I'm planning
on eating three slices of pizza plus a smoothie. I
hope that Aunt Sandra and Uncle Evon are okay with
that!

A waitress with bouncy, fiery-red, pigtails greets
us.

"Welcome to Pami's Pizzeria! What can I do for
you?" she asks.

"We'd like a table for three please," Aunt
Sandra requests.

"Of course! I'll be right back!" the girl exclaims
as she goes to clean off a table and set it.

We wait for a couple of minutes, and she comes
back. The table she set is sparkly-clean. Boy, she's
fast! I notice that not many people have shown up to
eat here tonight.

We sit down and take out our napkins to put on our laps. We also start looking at the menus.

"So, can we order now?" Uncle Evon asks in a few minutes.

"You're hungry aren't you, Uncle Evon?" I ask.

His cheeks redden.

"I'll have a cheese pizza," I announce.

"Don't you want to try something new, dear?" Aunt Sandra asks.

"No. I like cheese," I reply.

"Okay, one cheese. What do you want, Sandra?" Uncle Evon asks Aunt Sandra.

"I'll have a Neapolitan pizza," she replies.

"Nice. I'll have a pineapple and olive pizza," Uncle Evon says.

He waves his hand in the air. I guess that's what they do in restaurants to get the waitress' attention.

"Are you ready to order? asks a different girl with a perfect, jet-black bun. She was also polite.

"We would like a cheese pizza, a Neapolitan pizza, and a pineapple and olive pizza please," Uncle Evon says.

"Okay. Would you like extra cheese on the cheese pizza?" she asks.

Uncle Evon looks at me.

"No, thank you," I reply to the waitress.

"So, one cheese pizza, one Neapolitan pizza, and a pineapple and olive pizza. Is that all?" she asks.

"For now, yes," Uncle Evon says.

"Righto. Your food will be ready in about half an hour," she tells us.

And now we're waiting patiently - correction - we're starving!

At last, the waitress comes back with the pizza. It's delicious. After we finish, our stomachs are super-full.

"Got room for dessert?" Uncle Evon asks.

"Definitely!" I exclaim.

I have a huge sweet-tooth and always save some space for dessert.

Uncle Evon looks at Aunt Sandra.

"I don't know..." she replies, unsure.

"Pretty please with a cherry on top!" Uncle Evon and I convince.

"Enjoy yourselves!" she says.

"I want a cookies and cream smoothie," I tell Uncle Evon, after we browse through the dessert menu.

"Sure. I'll have a cup of mango sorbet. What about you, Sandra?" Uncle Evon asks.

"I'll have a low-fat almond milkshake," Aunt Sandra replies.

Uncle Evon calls for a waitress again. It's the one with the red pigtails this time.

"How can I help you?" she asks.

"Could we please have a cookies and cream smoothie, a cup of mango sorbet, and a low-fat almond milkshake?" Uncle Evon asks.

"You betcha! I'll be right back with your desserts," she replies as she enters the door that has "KITCHEN (STAFF ONLY)" on it.

We don't have to wait for long because within ten minutes she brought our desserts.

We finish them in a jiffy, Uncle Evon pays the bill, and we're on our way home in our car.

When we get home, I have some time to do further investigations with the pendulum. I finish most of my homework in the car-ride home. All I have left is science.

I take the pendulum out of my sky-blue backpack and place it on my hickory-brown desk, in my room. I do so many investigations, testing the pendulum out with a million different objects and variables.

Eventually Aunt Sandra comes to my room in her pajamas. That's when I check the time. It's past midnight! Time really does fly!

She yawns and says, "Go to bed, Ella. You have school tomorrow."

I have completed all the investigations in the worksheet and a bunch of extra ones, so I listen to her words.

CHAPTER 3
DREAMS DAY

"The mind is the limit. As long as the mind can envision the fact that you can do something, you can do it."- Arnold Schwarzenegger

Somehow, I manage to wake up on time in the morning! I know that luck alone has to save me from being late for school today. Most kids are in homeroom, while I haven't even left home yet.

When I'm putting on my shoes, I hear the telephone ringing.

"I'll get it!" I holler as I walk to the tiny table with our burgundy-red telephone on it, while wearing only one of my robin-egg-blue slip-ons, thinking someone is calling about something urgent.

"Who is it?" I ask once I pick up the telephone.

"It's me," the voice which I can tell is Cari replies.

"What is it, Cari?" I ask.

"Guess what? Today, we don't have any classes," she tells me.

"Are you sure this isn't some false info?" I ask.

"100% sure! Apparently, today's this weird school event called Dreams Day," she half-explains.

"What in the world is that?" I ask.

"Get over here. You'll see," she replies as she hangs up.

Sometimes Cari can be annoying like that. I decide to walk - no - run to school after saying bye to Aunt Sandra and Uncle Evon. I'm not really one for running, but I'd rather run than be late for school.

Panting, I reach homeroom exactly one minute before school starts.

I immediately go to Cari and Milly's desks and ask, "Why did you suddenly hang-up?"

"Life is better with surprises here and there, Ella," Cari says, in her wise voice.

I can clearly tell that's an excuse.

Right as I'm about to say something, our homeroom teacher, Mr. Merrin tells us, "Ella, Cari, Milly, you have an assembly to go to."

"Sorry," we all apologize at the same time and walk out of the room, to the auditorium.

Once we get there, our principal, Mrs. Willford is up on the podium, holding a microphone.

To tell you a bit about her, Mrs. Willford has gray hairs here and there, but she's still generally fit.

Also, I should warn you, she's kind of short-tempered.

"Everyone, please stay standing," she announces.

Some kids are talking with their friends.

"And silent!" she adds, angrily.

Within milliseconds, the room was of total silence.

"Thank you. Today is not a normal day. It is Dreams Day. Dreams Day is a new school event that our middle school has decided to pilot. It is a day when you will have the chance to think about your dreams for your future. It is not just thinking, though. You will be in groups of three and all three of you will be discussing your dreams until lunch. After lunch, you will spend a meaningful amount of time writing what you learnt about the different dreams in your group. Oh, and if you have not realized already, all classes have been canceled today. Please raise your hand if anything I have said so far is not clear," she tells us.

Not one hand went up. Mrs. Willford explains things like this well.

"Also, you don't get to pick the groups."

Did she really have to say that?

I want to be in a group with Cari and Milly, and they do too because we whisper-whine. This is a dreaded moment for all students in case you didn't know. There's a lot of groaning, moaning, and downright complaining.

"Enough! I know that everyone likes choosing groups, but it's better if we assign the groups to keep things from getting chaotic. So, please be quiet!" she yells.

All the students quiet down.

"Mr. Simson will be announcing the groups," she says as she hands the microphone to our associate principal, Mr. Simson.

Mr. Simson is a middle-aged man. I'm not trying to be mean or anything, but he has only a piece of hair on his head and is basically bald.

"Hello, students. I hope you are all doing good. I will now read out the group assignments, listen carefully," he starts.

I forgot to say that he has a deep voice.

"Group one is Suhanya, Cari, and Travis," he says.

Not too bad for Cari.

"Group two is Milly, Remar, and Boris," he adds.

It's okay for Milly.

"Group three is Savanna, Rye, and Ella," he says.

My group is bad. Plain bad. Savanna is one of the cool but mean girls from seventh grade. We've never really talked to each other, but I've seen how she can be cruel. And Rye is one of those boys who do things that are not smart to fit in the crowd. He's from eighth grade. Both of them go to detention a lot.

This is going to be my worst nightmare!

"The first three groups can go meet and head to wherever your group wants to go. Though please stay within the school," Mr. Simson tells us.

I go to Savanna.

"Why are *you* here?" she asks.

What a diva!

"I'm in your group," I grind my molars.

"Ugh, fine." she replies.

Rye's dilly-dallying by talking to his "crowd".

I walk over to him, and say, "Excuse me, Rye."

"'Sup," he replies.

"You need to come."

"Alrighty," he replies as he follows me to Savanna.

Luckily, he's nice, or I'm toast.

"Where do you want to go?" I ask as we all get together.

"I say we go to the lunchroom," Rye suggests.

"Eh, okay," Savanna agrees.

"Fine by me," I chime in.

We head to the lunchroom which is inconveniently located on the other side of school. In our elementary school, the gym and lunchroom are back-to-back. The elementary school commons is literally one large room, with a divider-wall in the middle.

We finally reach the lunchroom. The smell of spaghetti and marinara sauce filled the air. Spaghetti and marinara sauce would outweigh continuous PB&J, any day.

"I call dibs on this table," Rye announces.

"You do realize that there is no one here and that you don't need to call dibs now, right?" Savanna asks.

"Yep, force of habit," he admits.

That's when I notice that he is already seated at a table.

Savanna and I walk to the table.

42

I sit down.

"Savanna, would you mind sitting down?" I ask.

"This table's filthy," Savanna complains as she points to a weird stain on the bench.

"Sit down, Ms. Fussy Pants," Rye replies.

"Hmmph," she scoffs as she goes over to grab a napkin to wipe her bench with.

"Okay. Who wants to go first?" I ask once Savanna finishes acting like Ms. Fussy Pants.

"Me! My dream to become a famous celebrity," Savanna replies.

I predicted she was going to say something along the lines of that!

"Nice," I lie.

"I'll go next. My dream is to be a video-game creator," Rye says.

"Cool," I comment, this time telling the truth.

"What about you?" he asks me.

I haven't actually thought about my dream, but that's when I realize what mine is.

"My dream is to create time-travel. Einstein came up with the concept and I'm going to follow it," I reply, with confidence.

They immediately burst into laughter. My face turns red.

"Excuse me," I say.

"Are you crazy? Time travel's impossible," Savanna tells me.

"Yeah. You're out of your mind," Rye adds.

It takes me a long while to decide on how I should respond to that.

"Well, I don't care what you two think," I reply.

"Fine, but everyone I know thinks what we think. Look," Savanna says, pointing to her rose-gold phone, covered with rhinestones.

I look at the screen. There's a social media page. Savanna has made a poll. The question on the screen asks, "Is time-travel impossible?" and according to the replies, hundreds of Savanna's friends have said yes within seconds. Oh, so that was what she was doing with her phone. I should have known better.

"You have social media, plus so many friends, and they all reply so fast?" I ask.

"Yep, yep, and yep," she replies.

"My friends probably think that too. I mean anyone who hears about your idea will think that you're silly," Rye says.

I go silent for the rest of the time. Rye and Savanna rant on and on about their dreams, and I listen.

RING-RING-RING! Wow, for once I'm relieved that it's lunchtime.

I go to my locker, grab the tortilla-brown sack with my lunch in it, and walk to the lunchroom.

When I reach the table that Cari, Milly, and I usually sit at, I notice that my friends are not there yet. I guess that they are still with their groups. I place my sack on the table and sit down. Then, I start eating.

A couple minutes later, Milly and Cari arrive along with their groups, unlike me. Right when the lunch-bell rang, Rye, Savanna, and I split up. Milly and Cari are smiling as they reach the table. Immediately, their facial expressions change.

"Ella, what happened?" Cari asks.

"Nothing," I reply.

"Ella, we know you. You're making the face you make when you're trying your hardest not to cry. Just tell us what's going on," Milly says.

If there's one thing my friends are good at, it's probing.

"Okay. I told Rye, and Savanna about my dream to create time-travel, and they made fun of it. That really hurt my feelings," I reply.

I realize that I sound like a little kid, but I don't care about that, there are bigger things on my mind right now.

"I'm gonna give those two a piece of my mind," Milly grunts, acting all tough.

Milly is nice, but if something is not right, she fights for it!

"Calm down, Milly. Did you tell them how you feel, Ella?" Cari asks.

"No, that's not going to help," I explain.

I can't believe that they don't understand that I'm dealing with the meanest kids in school.

"Yeah, Cari. Ella, we believe in you. If you want to create time-travel, you go, girl!" Milly cheers.

"You can do it, Ella!" Cari motivates.

"Thanks, guys. You're the best!" I reply.

We group-hug.

After lunch, I get back with my group, and I'm miserable. The only thing that isn't so bad is that we need to just write instead of talk. I grab a paper and head back to *my* table. After all, there's not any rule saying that we have to sit together.

I finish filing the paper out, super-fast. I'm assuming that Rye and Savanna are done, too. Savanna is taking selfies of herself, and Rye is doodling weird things on the back of his paper. Then, Mrs. Willford makes an announcement on the intercom.

"Boys, and girls, when you're done writing about the dreams in your group, please share what you wrote down with your group members," Mrs. Willford requests.

More groupwork, great. A big pile of regret follows me as I walk to Savanna's table and sit down. Rye joins us.

"I'll go first. A good thing about Savanna's dream is how it reflects her personality. A good thing about Ella's dream is its craziness. Here are some visual aids," Rye says as he points to two drawings.

The first one is of a glamorous face and showing that it equals Savanna. The second one is of a crazy face labeled with my name! So hurtful!

"My turn. A good thing about Rye's dream is how it includes something of his interests. A good thing about Ella's dream is its weirdness. Here are my visual aids," Savanna says as she points to her drawings.

The first one is a video gaming face and showing that relates to Rye. The second one is of a weird face with spinning eyes and its tongue sticking out, and it's me again!

"Oh, you both did almost the same thing. How nice," I reply, sarcastically.

Why didn't I think of it?! I bet that they planned it ahead of time to make me feel bad. Oh, wait a minute! They're Rye and Savanna. They don't have to plan on being mean. It just comes naturally.

"My turn. A good thing about Savanna's dream is that it is big. A good thing about Rye's dream is how he wants his future to be about what he enjoys doing. I haven't made any visual aids, though," I say.

50

"Okay. There's still thirty more minutes until school ends," Rye replies as he runs off.

Savanna leaves as well.

They leave me alone and isolated. I put my head down on the table. This is officially the worst day of my life!

In a few seconds, I lift up my head. Two can play at that game! I should just go somewhere and enjoy myself like how Rye and Savanna are probably doing right now! If I had thought of it when they were leaving, that would have been cooler.

But anyways, I have always wanted to go to Mr. Peso's science room, and just hang out with him. I've always wanted to just talk to him, not about anything school-related, but I've never been able to find any time.

I walk to Mr. Peso's science room, crossing my fingers, hoping that he's there.

"Hey, Ella. What're you doing here?" he asks as I enter the room.

"Hi, Mr. Peso. I just want to hang out here," I reply.

"Aren't you supposed to be with your group doing Dreams Day related things?" he asks.

"We're done. I'm not asking much, but is it okay if I stay in here for a while?" I ask.

"Sure, you can stay!" he exclaims, "And if it's not too much trouble, would you mind wiping the outsides of the terrariums?"

Mr. Peso has terrariums full of animals in his room. That's one of the things I like most about it. They're full of all sorts of critters. I'm happy to clean them.

"Of course!" I reply.

He hands me a spray-bottle, full of some cleaning liquid and a rag, like the ones that they used to wipe off tables in the lunchroom. I immediately get to work, though it doesn't seem like work at all! I feel all warm and fuzzy like I'm doing a good deed. I clean all four sides of all the terrariums thoroughly. Within minutes, I'm done.

"Done!" I say as I hand Mr. Peso the spray-bottle and rag.

He looks at the terrariums and praises me, "You're so fast, Ella! They're squeaky clean!"

I feel proud as I look back at the shine on each one of the terrariums. And is it just me, or are the critters inside the terrariums smiling at me?

"May I just hang around here now?" I ask Mr. Peso.

After all, that was the main purpose of my coming to the science room.

"Why not? You're free to do whatever you want," he replies.

Just then, the bell rings. School's over.

"See you later, Mr. Peso!" I wave.

"Bye, Ella!" he replies.

It may seem like what I just did was a waste of time, but as long as I am helping get some of the load off one of my hardworking teachers' backs, that's all that matters.

CHAPTER 4
SHOCKING NEWS

"When you believe that you can do something, that's when you can." - Joseph Gordon-Levitt

What happened with Rye and Savanna on Tuesday was bad enough, but yesterday we got extra homework to cover for missed learning. Luckily, lots of kids complained about their troubles because of Dreams Day and Mrs. Willford decided to call this an unsuccessful piloting experience. So, we won't have another Dreams Day ever again. Yay!

It's Thursday. I just came home. I decide to go to the kitchen and grab a snack because I'm starving, and dinner is not ready yet. I go downstairs and walk to the kitchen. As I enter the kitchen (there's no door, but you know what I mean), I look around for something that looks good. I take an apple from the fruit bowl. That's when I realize that Aunt Sandra, and Uncle Evon are working in their shared office room that's attached to the kitchen in a way.

"Ella, we have something we need to tell you," Aunt Sandra says as they both walk into the kitchen.

"What is it?" I ask.

"Your wonderful friend, Jia, is coming to visit from Italy. Her flight is arriving on Saturday afternoon. She is going to stay here for the weekend. And you're happy to share your room with her," Uncle Evon replies.

"Say what?" I ask, with astonishment.

Jia is my infuriating "friend". Aunt Sandra and Uncle Evon are friends with her parents. She always wows everyone, acting like an angel. She gets on my nerves *all* the time. For some reason, everyone adores her. When we get together, we have competitions after competitions. We have not met in five years. When we last met, we had a eat-the-donuts-on-the-string-with-no-hands competition. She purposefully kicked me, so that she would win. I face-planted right onto the grass. Thankfully, none of my bones broke. I just got a bruise on my nose. She blamed it on my clumsiness and impressed the parents with her first-aid skills that she used on me. I tried telling everyone that she pushed me, but she just said that I'm jealous. I wasn't a single bit jealous. Who could be jealous of that pain in the neck? And she got away with it! Now, I have to share my room with her. Come on, people!

"She can't!" I cry.

"And give me one good reason why, young lady," Aunt Sandra demands.

"Uh…Cari and Milly are coming over for a sleepover on Saturday and my room isn't big enough for four people," I lie.

"Did you check with me about it?" Aunt Sandra asks.

I shake my head.

"Well, can't Jia stay in another room?" I ask.

"No. We only have so many rooms in our house," Uncle Evon replies.

There are only three bedrooms in this house. One is Aunt Sandra and Uncle Evon's room. One is my room. We use one as a storage room. I say that the architects should have built a bigger house, or Aunt Sandra and Uncle Evon should have bought a bigger one.

"Can't she sleep on the couch?" I ask.

Aunt Sandra grimaces.

"But…but…," I stammer.

"Show a little hospitality. It's just one, measly weekend," Uncle Evon replies.

"The decision is final. No more talking about it," Aunt Sandra, strictly.

Winning an argument with adults is hard. They always know what points to use at what time in the argument. Even without any practice in debates, they are masters. I wonder why. Probably experience.

I walk up to my room with an apple. I don't even know why I brought it with me, since this whole calamity made me lose my appetite!

CHAPTER 5
WELCOME, JIA!

"I will not let anyone walk through my mind with their dirty feet."- Mahatma Gandhi

The next day, I wake up undeniably late.

When I reach the living room, Aunt Sandra, and Uncle Evon are sitting on the couch, watching the news.

"Good morning, Ella," Uncle Evon says as he notices me.

"Good morning," I reply, yawning.

"Ella, you shouldn't wake up this late. It's bad for your health. You have to go to sleep and wake up at the right time every day," Aunt Sandra scolds.

"Loosen up, Sandra. It's no biggie to oversleep one day," Uncle Evon says.

We have hash browns and eggs for brunch. I called for an emergency meeting yesterday at lunch to ask Cari and Milly for some advice on how to deal with Jia. They were completely blank, so I just decided to be nice to her and hope for the best.

"I've decided that I'm going to be nice to Jia when she's here," I reply.

"That's the attitude! We knew you had that generosity in you!" Uncle Evon says, happily.

"Do you have Jia's gift ready?" he asks Aunt Sandra.

"Sorry. I've been so occupied with managing all the agents that I've not found time to go shopping," Aunt Sandra apologizes.

"I think we have a girls' make-up kit. Ella, could you please get it, it's upstairs in the storage room?" she asks.

"On it!" I reply as I run to the storage room.

I see that it's bigger than when I last came here. I struggle to get to the make-up boxes. A few days after I was adopted, Aunt Sandra bought a bunch of make-up kits from the section in the back of Bitti's Beauty Boutique for me. I was just three years old. We hadn't really met a lot before that, so they didn't know much about me.

When she came home, she called me, "Ella, I have gifts for you!"

I put on a confused face.

"They're make-up kits for children!" she replied, with a gleaming smile.

"Make-up kits yucky!" I said, sticking my tongue out.

"Uh, what?" Aunt Sandra asked, looking hurt.

I was young, so I didn't know that I had to say sorry. Instead, I ran away. I don't know why or how, but ever since I was little, I've always disliked make-up.

My mom never wore make-up - at least she isn't wearing any in the photos. I have very few memories of my parents. I know that my mom's name was Katrene, she had orange-golden hair, and had the most beautiful voice. She was very sweet and gentle. She's Aunt Sandra's big sister, but nothing like her. Meanwhile, my dad, Lawrence, was simple. He had caramel-brown hair that was always parted perfectly, fair skin, and a mysterious scar on his forehead. I miss my parents so much!

I almost forget the whole reason I came up here until Aunt Sandra asks, "Are you okay, Ella? What's taking so long?"

"I'm fine. I'll be there in a second," I reply as I quickly grab a make-up kit, and rush downstairs.

As I reach the living room, I hand Aunt Sandra the make-up kit.

"Oh, look at the time. I'd better get going if I want to pick up Jia on time," Uncle Evon says.

Aunt Sandra sends me off to get my room ready for Jia. I sweep, vacuum, and arrange. I finish in no time.

"Looking good!" Aunt Sandra exclaims from the doorway.

I hadn't even realized that she was there.

"Thanks," I reply.

"And I'm sorry. We should have asked you before we told Jia's parents that she could stay in your room," she apologizes.

"I'm sorry, too. I'll put aside our differences and be kind to Jia when she gets here."

"Best niece ever!" she says.

"Best aunt ever!" I reply.

We hug for a long time.

Just then, the doorbell rings. We walk downstairs and open the door. I see Uncle Evon and Jia standing there, and Jia's mound of luggage is behind them. It's probably going to take up most of my room!

"Hi!" Jia says.

"Welcome, Jia!" we reply.

"How was your flight?" Aunt Sandra asks.

"Exhausting!" Jia replies.

"Go on up to Ella's room and rest then. Ella will take you there," Aunt Sandra says.

"What about my suitcases?" Jia asks.

"Oh, don't you worry about that. I'll bring them up," Uncle Evon replies.

We walk to my room and Uncle Evon follows.

Once it's only me and her, she exclaims, "Ella, I'm so happy to be here! Let's forget about the past and have fun!"

Wow, I guess she turned over a new leaf.

I remember that I need to do my homework, but I'll have plenty of time after dinner. Besides, you aren't a procrastinator if you just put something off once, right?

"What do you want to do?" I ask.

"Give each other make-overs!" she replies.

Not in a million years would I do that, but Jia's the guest, and to be a good hostess, I've got to go along with what she says.

"Okay. Let's go ask Aunt Sandra for some make-up. She's got tons!" I reply.

We dash downstairs to the office room where Aunt Sandra is typing something on her laptop.

"Aunt Sandra, can we have make-up?" I ask.

"Of course! Why?" she asks.

"We want to give each other make-overs," Jia replies.

"Oh, I loved doing that with my childhood friends. We had so much fun! I'll be back in a second!" she exclaims.

She comes back with a make-up box.

"Feel free to use whatever's in here," she says as she hands us the box.

"Thanks!" we both reply.

We go back to my room and open the box. We see all kinds of make-up and get started.

20 minutes later...

It took time, and work, but we're finally done putting make-up on each other.

"We look awful!" we exclaim, looking in my vanity mirror.

We laugh but stop as we hear the clicks you hear when you're taking photos. Aunt Sandra, and Uncle Evon are standing outside of my room taking photos of us on their phones.

"You two look so funny!" they say.

"Is that bad?" Jia asks.

"Well, are you two having fun?" Aunt Sandra asks.

"Yeah!" we exclaim.

"Then that's all that matters!" Aunt Sandra replies.

"Hey, speaking of fun, who wants to play some games?" Uncle Evon asks.

"I do!" we all reply.

CHAPTER 6
MEAN CHEF IN THE HOUSE!

"You can do anything you wish to do, have anything you wish to have, be anything you wish to be."-
Robert Collier

We play so many games and time just seems to pass.

"How do you know so many games?" I ask.

"Before TV was popular, families used to spend a lot of time together. Our families taught us a lot of games!" Uncle Evon replies.

"That's so cool! But how do you seem to remember all the rules and stuff for every, single game?" Jia asks.

"If you played as much as we did, you're sure to remember!" Aunt Sandra laughs.

"I think that's it for now," Uncle Evon says.

Aunt Sandra says, "Yes, it's time for dinner. I'll go warm up some leftover pasta."

The truth is, throughout the games, I felt uneasy because of my lie. I realize that I must tell Aunt Sandra, and Uncle Evon the truth.

"Aunt Sandra, Uncle Evon, I lied to you," I reveal.

"Wait, what did you just say?" Uncle Evon asks.

"Sorry, but actually I have homework to do. I postponed it because I wanted to have fun," I reply.

"Ella, you know that you have to finish your homework before doing anything else. I still can't believe you would do something like this," Aunt Sandra says.

"I know, I'm so sorry," I apologize.

"I'm disappointed in you. We'll talk about your punishment later. Go and do your homework," Uncle Evon replies.

I trudge to my room when Aunt Sandra announces, "Dinner will be ready in just a bit."

"You said we're having pasta, right?" Jia asks.

Aunt Sandra nods.

"I've been taking cooking lessons. I can help you make a gravy to go with the pasta. It tastes really good," Jia offers.

"That would be kind of you, but you're the guest, I don't want to give you any trouble," Aunt Sandra replies.

"No trouble at all! I'm glad to help!" Jia exclaims.

A few minutes later, I hear the stove turning on. That's when I remember that I'm supposed to do my homework and not eavesdrop. I zoom to my bedroom and grab my backpack with my salmon-pink binder in it. I look at my planner. I have a math worksheet on writing algebraic equations along with a reading on Helen Keller.

It isn't too bad. It's a good thing that we only get math and ELA homework on the weekends because otherwise I would have a handful of things to do. Before I know it, I'm done!

"Dinner is ready!" Aunt Sandra calls.

"Coming!" I reply.

When I reach the dining room, Aunt Sandra and Jia are setting the table. The aroma of the gravy is surprisingly good.

"Are you done with your homework?" Uncle Evon asks from the couch.

"Yep. I'm done with all of it," I reply.

"Good. Everyone take your seats," Aunt Sandra tells us.

She puts some penne pasta on all the plates and pours the crimson-red gravy too. We all start eating our food.

Jia deserves a point for this!

"How do you know this recipe?" Aunt Sandra asks Jia.

"I was just experimenting with gravy one day in cooking class and it worked," Jia replies.

"You're brilliant!" Uncle Evon tells her.

"You don't need to praise me so much. I just made a gravy. Anyone can do that," Jia says.

"This isn't ordinary, it's exceptional! Have you ever thought of becoming a chef?" Aunt Sandra asks.

"That's a great idea, but I have other plans for my future," Jia replies.

"What plans?" Uncle Evon asks.

Even though there is improvement in her, I'm sure the bragging is still there.

"I want to be a stylist," Jia replies, not boastfully.

"That's nice!" Aunt Sandra and Uncle Evon reply.

She has changed! She's humble.

"What do you want to do in your future, Ella?" Jia asks.

"I want to create time-travel," I reply.

She is as quiet as a mouse.

"So…?" I ask.

"That is absurd! Time-travel isn't real, duh!" Jia snorts.

"It is! Einstein's theory proves it!" I try to defend myself.

"Miss Einstein! Miss Einstein!" she jeers.

Yep. Jia's true colors are starting to show.

I don't know what to say, so I childishly run to my room.

I hear Aunt Sandra cry, "Ella, wait! We can talk this out!"

I bury my face deep in my pillow and have a meltdown.

Why do so many people think time-travel will never work?

As Aunt Sandra approaches my room, she asks, "What's the matter?"

"What's the matter? Really? So many people don't support me in my dream of creating time-travel. All of them put me down!" I reply.

"So many people? Just Jia, right? Who else?" Aunt Sandra asks.

I tell her about Rye and Savanna.

"You could have told us about this earlier, we're here to help," she replies.

"I know, I'm sorry," I apologize.

"It's okay. Now back on Jia, I'm going to give her a stern talking to," Aunt Sandra says.

Aunt Sandra and I return to our seats and she tells Jia, "What you did was wrong, Jia. You shouldn't make fun of anyone's dreams."

"I'm sorry, Ella," Jia replies, but I can tell she doesn't mean it.

After a while, "So, what plans do we have for tomorrow?" I ask.

"It's Jia's choice. Jia, where do you want to go? The beach? The museum?" Aunt Sandra asks.

"Or do you want to go down-town? There are plenty of sights to see there. How does that sound?" Uncle Evon asks.

"I was thinking we can just spend time together like today and maybe eat out," Jia replies.

We agree on that. But I know that's not what she really wants to do. She's just trying to impress Aunt Sandra, and Uncle Evon with her simplicity, obviously!

CHAPTER 7
NEW CUISINE

"The most important thing is to believe in yourself and know that you can do it." - Gabby Douglass

I wake up to an incredibly cacophonous noise.

"Huh, what? Did the smoke detector just go off?" I ask, barely awake.

"No, silly goose! It's just me trying to wake you up," Jia replies.

I notice that she's already dressed. I also see that it is 10 o'clock in the morning. I go brush my teeth.

Jia hands me a honey-nut granola bar for breakfast. She knows I don't like them! But my hunger makes me gobble it up.

"I'll go shower," I tell Jia.

I take a quick shower.

Aunt Sandra always advises, "If there is even the slightest chance of being photographed, wear nice clothes. It's better to be safe than sorry!"

Today, we might take photos as memories and I don't want to look bad, so I change into a neat watermelon-pink T-Shirt along with a lime-green and arctic-blue patterned capri.

"Hurry up! We don't have all day!" Uncle Evon calls.

"I'll be right there!" I reply as I go meet Aunt Sandra, Uncle Evon, and Jia in the living room.

"What are we going to do today?" I ask.

We all look at Jia.

"Let's just stay home," Jia replies.

"Are you sure there's *nothing* else that you want to do?" Uncle Evon asks.

Jia nods.

"What do you want to do here?" Aunt Sandra asks.

"What do you usually do on Sundays at home?" Jia asks.

"Not much," I reply.

"Just tell me what you do," Jia says.

"We go to the backyard and have a picnic when the weather is nice," I reply.

"Let's do it!" Jia exclaims.

We pack the picnic basket with salad, cheese and vegetable paninis, chips, lemonade, and cupcakes (for dessert).

"I guess we're all set!" Aunt Sandra says.

Aunt Sandra, Jia, and I put on our sandals and walk outside while Uncle Evon heaves the picnic basket as he follows us.

He looks worn out as he throws himself on the hammock we got at a garage sale last summer.

"Are you okay?" Jia and I ask at the same time.

"That thing is heavy! But I'm fine. Thanks for asking," he replies.

Aunt Sandra places the picnic-blanket on the grass and lays out all the food. We sit down. She places some salad and a panini along with some chips on each of our plates. She pours some lemonade into our cups as well. Clearly, we're all famished. We quickly wolf down the food.

"Ready for dessert?" Uncle Evon asks as we finish our food.

"Oh, yeah!" I reply.

Aunt Sandra sets a cupcake on each of our plates. They're berry cupcakes. Yum! As we finish, we pack everything back into the picnic basket and just sit there, in absolute quietude.

"What are we going to do now?" I ask.

"Can we watch a movie?" Jia asks.

"Of course!" Uncle Evon replies.

"Yay!" Jia says.

"What kind of movies do you watch?" I ask.

"All kinds," Jia replies.

"Okay. I'll look for a good movie," Uncle Evon says as he browses on his phone.

"Can we have popcorn?" I ask.

Aunt Sandra always has a tub of popcorn kernels in the pantry.

"Are you sure? We just ate lunch," Aunt Sandra replies.

"I know, but for some reason I'm hungry," I say.

Jia agrees.

Aunt Sandra fills a pot with popcorn kernels and oil. She puts the pot on the stove.

She puts the lid on the pot and says, "It shouldn't take long."

"Uncle Evon, have you found a movie yet?" I ask.

"As a matter of fact, I have," Uncle Evon replies.

"What movie is it?" Jia asks.

"It's called 'Pear Tree'. It looks good!" Uncle Evon tells us.

"Could you please check the reviews?" Aunt Sandra asks Uncle Evon.

"Why do you ALWAYS check the reviews? Reviews are just opinions. And different people have different opinions. Just because someone writes a review saying that a movie is bad you shouldn't believe that it is - or rather that you won't like it," I reply.

"Wow. That was one moving speech," Uncle Evon says.

"Agreed. It persuaded me to make this decision: I will listen to what I think about something instead of reading others' reviews from now on," Aunt Sandra chimes in.

"Thank you, Uncle Evon. And I would have never thought that I would be able to help you make that decision, Aunt Sandra," I reply.

"Sorry to interrupt this conversation, but can we start the movie?" Jia asks.

"Sure," we all chorus.

Jia and I lounge on the couch while Aunt Sandra puts the heavenly popcorn in a big bowl and Uncle Evon connects his phone to the TV and starts the movie.

We finish watching the movie and it's around 4:30 PM (we started at about 3 PM). It was an amazing movie about a man who travels around the world with his treasured pear tree, but don't worry, it's way more interesting than that.

A while after the movie started, when Aunt Sandra reached for some popcorn all she felt was some powder and kernels, "I regret not making more," she said.

For a while, we have time for some pure relaxation. Now it's 6:05.

Jia asks, "Is it okay if we eat a home-cooked dinner?"

"Sure. But I thought you wanted to eat out. What happened?" Uncle Evon asks.

"Nothing. It's just that I'm not too hungry and I want to eat at home. I hope it's okay," Jia replies.

"Totally okay! But since this is unplanned, I don't know what to cook. Do you have any ideas?" Aunt Sandra asks Jia.

"We should cook something from a different cuisine. I suggest Indian. It's delicious!" Jia replies.

"Hey, you know how to cook Indian food?" Uncle Evon asks.

I was about to ask the exact, same thing!

"My parents and I visited India and I learned how to cook a few dishes," Jia says.

"That sounds great! I love trying new things! Though I haven't cooked Indian food before. Could you please share the recipes?" Aunt Sandra asks.

"Of course, I can! We can make dosas and sambar. A dosa is a crispy pancake. And sambar is a lentil soup with vegetables. They are common Indian comfort foods! They taste so good together," Jia replies.

"Good idea, but I don't think we can pull the whole thing off with just the ingredients we have in the pantry, right?" Aunt Sandra asks, skeptically.

"You're right. We would need some dosa batter and sambar powder. It takes a long time to make dosa batter at home, but luckily many Indian grocery stores sell it premade. They have sambar powder, too. Are there any of those stores nearby?" Jia asks.

"I'm quite sure there is. There's this shopping complex near my office with an Indian grocery store called "Dila's Desi Dukaan". It looks good," Aunt Sandra replies.

"Okay. Let's make a quick stop there and buy the batter and powder," Uncle Evon says.

We rush to the car and Uncle Evon drives us there really close to the maximum speed limit.

It's 6:50 already. Shops close early on Sunday evenings. And I checked online, but the closing time wasn't listed.

"What if they're closed?" I ask.

"We'll just have to hope for the best," Uncle Evon replies.

Thankfully, we get there five minutes before the closing time. A woman greets us as we enter the store.

"Hello, I am Pooni. Welcome to Dila's Desi Dukaan. How may I help you?" she asks.

"Hi! I'm Sandra. Could you please help us get some premade dosa batter and sambar powder?" Aunt Sandra asks.

"Sure. One minute," Pooni replies as she walks further into the store.

She returns and says, "Here you go," as she hands Aunt Sandra a container filled to the top with dosa batter and some sambar powder in a package.

"Thank you!" Aunt Sandra exclaims.

"My pleasure," Pooni replies.

"Where do we pay?" Aunt Sandra asks.

Usually, the checkout area is in the front of the store, but it doesn't seem that way here.

"It is in the back of the store. Follow me," Pooni directs as she walks ahead.

At the very back of the store, we find the checkout area.

Pooni is the only person working right now, so she walks to one of the cashier's seats and sits down. She gestures for us to come on over. We walk over and Uncle Evon pays.

After the checkout process is over, Pooni says, "Thank you for shopping at Dila's Desi Dukaan. Have a great day!"

"You, too!" we all reply.

We come back home. It's 7:20 PM. Jia guides us through the process of making dosa and sambar.

"We're done!" she tells us after what seems like a million years.

I glance at the clock. It's nearly 9 PM. Aunt Sandra puts two dosas with some sambar on our plates. We dig in at once!

"Mmm! This is so good! The time and effort was worth it!" I say.

It's true, Jia and I don't get along, but this food is just too good!

"Agreed! This is just... wow. I've said this before and I'm saying this again: you should become a chef. You will rock!" Aunt Sandra applauds.

"Thanks!" Jia replies.

"I wish we could have you cook for us all the time," Uncle Evon jokes.

Jia smiles.

We rapidly finish eating. Later, we wash up and go upstairs where we brush our teeth and change into our pajamas. Having Jia sleep with me last night wasn't all that bad, but I would undoubtedly sleep by myself if I could. I'm relieved that she is going to leave tomorrow. I only have to deal with her for around 11 more hours. Freedom awaits!

CHAPTER 8
BAHAMAS, HERE WE COME!

"You can do anything you set your mind to."-
Benjamin Franklin

It's almost the end of 6th grade! Not much has changed. After all these years, Aunt Sandra, and Uncle Evon let me get a ZippeeMail account. ZippeeMail is a popular email company. But they still said I should get a child account.

I told them, "I'm not a child!"

"But you have to be at least 13 to have an adult account and you're not old enough," they replied.

"I'm 12. That's *almost* 13," I coaxed.

They didn't budge. And now they'll be watching over all the emails I send and receive until I'm 13. At times they're a bit too overprotective, but at least I have an email.

Also, sadly Cari, Milly, and I can't have electives together. It's because when it was my turn to choose what elective we all join; I chose the chemistry one (since there wasn't a physics one).

One day we were making a solution. Since we were zoning out, we randomly put substances into the beaker. You can probably guess what happened next. It exploded. In chemistry this happens all the time. If this was a normal explosion it would've been fine, but this was extreme. The teacher for that elective, Mr. Brux, is strict, so he told the electives head, Mrs. Liat, and she decided that the three of us should never be in another elective together again.

I'm just happy that we didn't get separated for all the classes. That would have been sad. Another thing: Cari, Milly, and I ride the public bus home now because we begged our parents to let us and they agreed – if we stay together at all times. We're on our way home right now.

The stop near my house is first. I get out of the bus and wave bye to my friends.

I eat string-cheese as my after-school snack and start on my homework. By the time, Aunt Sandra, and Uncle Evon get home I usually finish all my homework.

DING-DONG! Aunt Sandra and Uncle Evon are here. I open the door and let them in.

As they put down their things, Uncle Evon starts, "Ella, my friend Mauk is going to call any moment, so…"

"Wait, you're friends with Mauk as in Mauk Parei, the world-famous philanthropist, millionaire, and CEO of his web-design company *Starta*?" I ask, talking fast.

"Oh, yeah. Have I not told you about him?" Uncle Evon asks.

"Never," I reply.

"Oh, well like I was saying, he wants to call, so I can't talk for long," he says.

"Okay," I tell him.

Very soon, Uncle Evon gets a call.

"Hi, Evon," Mauk Parei says.

"Mauk, how are you, man?" Uncle Evon asks.

"Good. How about you, bro?" Mauk asks.

"I'm good, too. What's up?" Uncle Evon asks.

They catch up.

After a while, Mauk asks, "Would you and your family want to come and stay at my house for some time during summer break?"

"Are you sure it's okay?" Uncle Evon asks.

"Completely sure," Mauk replies.

"We'll think about it and let you know," Uncle Evon says.

"Okay. It was nice chatting, but I need to go now. Bye!" Mauk replies.

"Yeah, bye!" Uncle Evon tells him.

"Can we please go?" I ask.

"Ella, stop eavesdropping!" Uncle Evon replies.

"Hey! With how loud you two talk, you can't blame me," I say.

"Sandra!" Uncle Evon calls.

"Yes?" Aunt Sandra asks from upstairs.

"Could you please come over here a second?"
Uncle Evon asks.

Aunt Sandra comes downstairs.

"What is it?" she asks.

"You remember my best friend, Mauk, right?"
Uncle Evon asks.

Aunt Sandra nods.

"He invited the three of us to his house in the
Bahamas for summer break. Should we go?" Uncle
Evon asks.

"Why not? We all deserve a vacation. Your
school's out in two weeks, right, Ella?" Aunt Sandra
asks.

"Actually, it's two weeks and one day," I reply.

"Fine. Two weeks and one day, right?" she asks.

"Right," I tell her.

"Alright. I'll tell him," Uncle Evon says.

Just two more weeks and one day until our vacation! I can't wait!

CHAPTER 9
BON VOYAGE

"Just remember, you can do anything you set your mind to, but it takes action, perseverance, and facing your fears." - Gillian Anderson

Yes, yes, yes! The day is finally here! I've been counting down the days left for our trip. We rarely go on vacations so I'm ecstatic, but even still I'm going to try and contain myself.

It's been years since I've rode an airplane, but the ear-plugging feeling is unforgettable. This time I brought a pack of watermelon-flavored gum – I'm prepared.

Right now, we're sitting in our seats, ready-to-go. I feel the airplane shaking a little. All three of us put a piece of gum in our mouths and start chewing.

Take-off goes smoothly. I listen to a few songs and watch a movie on the passenger-screen, but after a while I'm so bored, I fall asleep.

When I wake up, I ask, "Are we there yet?"

Uncle Evon says no.

Apparently, it's just a powernap. And here's the weird thing about powernaps: when you wake up it feels like you've been asleep for a long time when it's only been five or ten minutes.

I wish I just stayed sleeping because now I'm not sleepy and I have nothing to do, so I have to wait.

Waiting is tough. Especially when you're impatient like me. I guess I have to learn patience if I want to become a scientist because scientists have to keep on trying with patience to succeed.

I look around and I'm glad to see flight-attendants passing out snacks and drinks.

When a flight-attendant gets to our seats, she asks us, "What snacks would you like?"

"What do you have?" we ask.

"Here's the snack menu. I'll take those guys' orders while you figure out what you want," she replies as she gives us the menu.

We look at it and I've never seen so many options! There are nachos, candy, and so much more!

Aunt Sandra wants a muffin and I want taco bites (they're mini tacos), and Uncle Evon wants cheese puffs.

The flight-attendant comes back to us and asks, "Have you made up your mind yet?"

"Yes, we have. A muffin for me, taco bites for her, and cheese puffs for him please," Aunt Sandra replies.

She hands each of us our snacks and asks, "Would you like any drinks?"

"Could you please come back to us?" Aunt Sandra asks, kind of embarrassed.

"Sure," the flight-attendant replies.

We look at the drink options on the drink menu which is on the back of the snack menu. There aren't that many choices, though. There's apple juice, orange juice, tomato juice, soda, and of course, water.

Aunt Sandra and Uncle Evon want apple juice and I want orange juice.

I don't want to bore you out because it's just going to be a couple more hours of monotony until we land at the Bahamas.

CHAPTER 10
AT MR. PAREI'S PLACE

"A genius shoots at something no one else can see, and hits it." - Holly Goldberg Sloan

Right now, we're riding home with Mauk. There are a lot of unexpected things about him like how he doesn't have a limo or driver and drives an ordinary car.

We're pulling up at his house and it is nothing like what I expected. It is just like our house. A normal, two-story house. My mouth is wide open in shock.

"You know, Ella, people are always surprised like you are when they see me," he says.

I apologize.

"No, no. You're fine. What I'm trying to say is that just because someone has a lot of money, doesn't mean that they need to spend it on a limo, driver, mansion, or any of those other fancy, unnecessary things. This is enough for my family," he replies.

"You're so wise, Mr. Parei," I say.

"And another thing: you don't need to treat me differently. I'm not a single bit more special than anyone else, really," he tells me.

"Okay," I reply.

We get out of the car and walk into his house. He gives us a tour. It's everything you could want in an average house.

"My wife, Shila, is out. She will be back in a few hours. You guys can get settled in. The guestroom is here," he tells us, pointing to a room.

Later, Mr. Parei calls, "Ella, can I talk to you for a second?"

"Uh, sure," I reply, not knowing how to react.

Why does Mauk Parei want to talk to me?

Downstairs, he gestures for me to come sit in the sage-green armchairs by the brunette-brown coffee table.

"Don't worry. I just wanted to listen to your perspective on things. I have already talked with my children and their friends. I want to know about your dream. Just that," he assures.

"My dream? Uh, uh, why?" I ask, stuttering.

"You seem like a very special kid. I believe that children now have amazing dreams, but don't get heard from," he says.

My dream. The words bring back so many horrible memories.

"Thank you, but I would prefer not to talk about that," I reply.

"Why? Have you not thought of your dream?" he asks.

"I have a dream, but it seems a tad *too* wild," I tell him.

That was the most polished way of saying that my dream is absolutely ridiculous!

"Well, let's hear it. If you ask me, there's no such thing as 'too wild'. Go on, Ella!" he encourages.

"My dream is to create time-travel just like Einstein's theory says," I say, not sounding very confident.

There was silence for a few seconds and then he replies, "Wow...I'm speechless, Ella. That is the most amazing dream ever!"

"It is?" I ask, flabbergasted.

"Yeah, it is just such an original and awesome dream!" he exclaims.

"I agree - if only it were more realistic," I reply.

"No, Ella, you're going about this the wrong way. Things that exist are considered *real*, but if you want to do something new and actually make a change, your idea doesn't need to be realistic," he points out.

"I want to create time-travel to answer many historical mysteries, but so many people oppose my dream though!"

"If you have such a great dream, obviously some people won't be keen about it, but that doesn't mean you should give up. Take it from me, when I was your age, I dreamed to design websites and make it possible for people to share things instantly. If I had stopped when people opposed me, I could not have helped everyone. Now, what do you think about your dream?" he asks.

"I guess it's pretty good," I reply.

"So, you're not going to give up, right?" he asks.

"No, I'll chase my dream," I tell him.

"I can't hear you!" he says.

"I will definitely chase my dream!" I say with joy.

"That's the spirit!"

I thank him for sending me the right way.

"Of course, Ella!" he replies.

I head upstairs and we relax a bit before Mauk's wife arrives. We have flatbread with vegetable curry for dinner and banana bread for dessert.

CHAPTER 11
LISTENING IN

"If you think you can do it, you can."- John Burroughs

After dinner, I head upstairs and just as I walk to the door of the guestroom, I hear Mr. Parei calling, "Evon, Sandra!"

"Yes?" they ask.

"Could I please talk to you guys a moment?" he asks.

"Yeah, sure," they reply, walking to the spruce-blue sectional sofa.

"Great. I wanted to talk to you about Ella," he tells them.

I was doubtful on whether I should be listening on the adults' conversation, but once Mr. Parei says my name, there is no doubt about it.

"What about her?" they ask, worried.

"It's nothing to stress about. I just learned about Ella's dream to create time-travel. Did you two know about that?" he asks.

Oh, so this is what it's about.

Uncle Evon nods.

"Yes, we do. Poor girl, she's been facing a lot of discouragement. Remember Jia and those other kids from school I told you about, Evon?" Aunt Sandra asks.

"Yep. I feel bad for her," Uncle Evon replies.

"Yes, I talked to her about that. But what I wanted to say is that she would benefit from experience in an actual lab, more than what she gets at school. Lab kits can help with that. Sorry if I am being a busybody," he apologizes.

"It's okay, we don't mind," Uncle Evon replies.

"Yeah, and I wish we could buy some lab kits for Ella and do more for her in general, but we can't afford it," Aunt Sandra cries, softly.

"We're having some tough times with work and even paying for all the necessities is a struggle nowadays. I'm not getting as many software projects as before because it's hard for me to learn new programs," Uncle Evon says, also slightly crying.

"And managing other real-estate agents is too hard," Aunt Sandra adds.

"Every day is a battlefield for us," they both say.

Watching them cry, tears well up in my eyes. I never knew that they had to face so many hardships every day.

"Please don't cry. I understand that these things are way more important than lab kits. I'd like to gift some lab kits to Ella. Please let me know if I can help you in other ways. It's no trouble," he assures.

They cry a bit more. I think they're feeling guilty that Mr. Parei is going to pay for something they are supposed to.

"You don't have to," they reply.

"I really want to," he insists.

They finally agree.

As they thank him, he exclaims, "Anytime!"

Mr. Parei has a heart of gold.

CHAPTER 12
30 YEARS IN THE FUTURE

"Only those who attempt the absurd can achieve the impossible."- Albert Einstein

"How is it possible, Ella?" my research assistant, Taea, asks.

It's just a usual Monday morning. We're in our physics lab where we work on time-travel research. Taea as usual asks a lot of questions. Even though I have to answer them, I really do enjoy her assistance and guiding her.

"How is what possible, Taea?" I ask.

"How are you so successful?" she asks.

"I'm not that successful," I reply.

"Don't be modest. You're the reason behind time-travel. You're the idol to so many people like me," she compliments.

I thank her, blushing.

I tell her, "Coming back to your question, just work hard and don't listen to any bad things other people tell you. There's no secret to success. I guess the experiences from my past did teach me a whole lot. As for the mean people, just because you come across a few mushy ones in a basket of tasty blueberries, you shouldn't throw them all away. There will always be bad people wherever you go - that's just life! But what you have to do is keep on going. Just keep chasing your dreams."

ABOUT THE AUTHOR

Akchara Mukunthu loves to write and interact with animals. She is also known as Author Betta. Check out her blog:

https://authorbetta.wixsite.com/thebettablog

Made in the USA
Monee, IL
02 January 2025

72862538R00075